All rights reserved. Published in the United States by Dragonfly Books, an imprint of Random House
Children's Books, a division of Random House, Inc., New York. Originally published in hardcover in
Great Britain by Julia MacRae Books, a division of Walker Books Limited, London, and subsequently in
hardcover in the United States by Alfred A. Knopf, an imprint of Random House Children's Books,
a division of Random House, Inc., New York, in 1989.

Dragonfly Books with the colophon is a registered trademark of Random House, Inc.

Visit us on the Web! www.randomhouse.com/kids

Educators and librarians, for a variety of teaching tools, visit us at
www.randomhouse.com/teachers

The Library of Congress has cataloged the hardcover edition of this work as follows:

Browne, Anthony.
Things I like.
Summary: A young chimp enumerates favorite playtime activities, from painting
and riding a bike to paddling in the sea and partying with friends.
ISBN 978-0-394-84192-2 (pbk.) — ISBN 978-0-394-94192-9 (lib. bdg.)
[1. Chimpanzees—Fiction. 2. Play—Fiction.] I. Title.
PZ7.B81984TTg 1989 [E] 88026632

MANUFACTURED IN CHINA
20 19 18 17 16 15 14 13

# Things
# I
# Like

## Anthony Browne

Dragonfly Books · New York

This is me
and this is what I like:

Painting...

and riding my bike.

Playing with toys,

and dressing up.

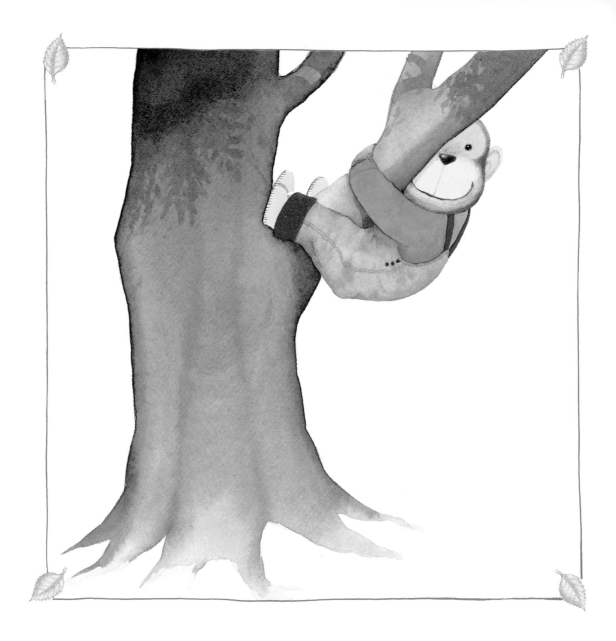

Climbing trees . . .

and kicking a ball.

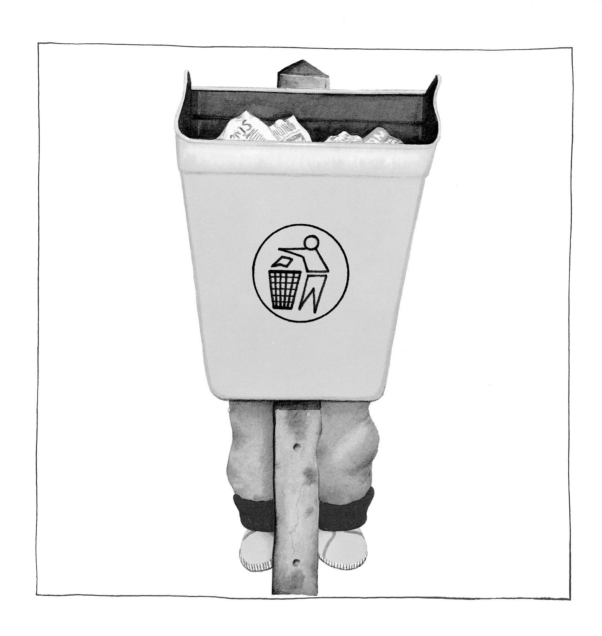

Hiding . . .

and acrobatics.

Building sandcastles,

and wading in the sea.

Making a cake . . .

and watching TV.

Going to birthday parties,

and being with my friends.

Having a bath . . .

...hearing a bedtime story...

and dreaming.